Little green BOOKS ™

I CAN SAVE THE EARTH!

By ALISON INCHES • Illustrated by VIVIANA GAROFOLI

LITTLE SIMON

An imprint of Simon & Schuster Children's Publishing Division

New York London Toronto Sydney

1230 Avenue of the Americas, New York, New York 10020

Text copyright © 2008 by Simon & Schuster, Inc.

Illustrations copyright © 2008 by Viviana Garofoli

Book design by Leyah Jensen

LITTLE SIMON is a registered trademark of Simon & Schuster, Inc., and

LITTLE GREEN BOOKS and associated colophons are trademarks of Simon & Schuster, Inc.

Manufactured in the United States of America

4 6 8 10 9 7 5 3

ISBN-13: 978-1-4169-6789-7 • ISBN-10: 1-4169-6789-3

0410 LAK

Max the Little Monster liked to fling candy wrappers. He left a trail of trash wherever he went. "Whee!" said Max.

Max the Little Monster did not like to give away his old toys—even when he'd outgrown them. "Mine!" cried Max.

Max the Little Monster liked to overflow the sink...

and the bathtub...
and clog the toilet.

"Hungry toilet!"
said Max.

Max the Little Monster
left the lights on and
blared the TV—even when he
wasn't in the room.

"No big **whoop**," said Max.

Then one night in the middle of his favorite program
something
unexpected
happened...

The lights went **out!**
And the TV went **off!**

There
had
been
a
BLACKOUT.

"Hey!" shouted Max. "Who turned out the lights?"
Max tripped over some old toys and
stumbled outside to see what was wrong.

Max looked around. He saw a full moon as it shone brightly on the colorful spring flowers.

He heard the crickets **chirp** and an owl **hoot**. He even saw a shooting star as it twinkled across the night sky!

"Wow," said Max. "This is so beautiful!"

When the lights came back on, Max the Little Monster felt something new. He began to notice things he hadn't noticed before.

In the summer Max the Little Monster went to the beach and noticed the pretty shells. He wiggled his toes in the sand. He watched the sun sparkle on the waves. He saw a dolphin leap out of the water.

Max picked up an old bottle and an ice-cream wrapper and threw them into a trash can.

"POLLUTION makes the beach look ugly," said Max. "And pollution can hurt animals and plants."

In autumn Max the Little Monster noticed the colorful leaves—red, orange, and yellow. He jumped in leaf piles with his friends.

"Leaves are so pretty—

and more fun to play in than watching TV!" cried Max.

After they jumped in the leaves, Max the Little Monster didn't want to leave a mess, so he COMPOSTED the leaves. "Rotten leaves help the dirt grow happy flowers," said Max.

In winter Max the Little Monster noticed the wonder of snowflakes. Each delicate snowflake looked like a crystal jewel.

He made a
T. rex...

an
igloo...

and a
Snow angel!

"Why didn't I see this before?"
wondered Max.
"The Earth is **beautiful!**"

Now Max the Little Monster never wastes water.
"More water—more snowflakes!" says Max.

And he **doesn't** waste toilet paper.

"Happy monster! Happy toilet! Happy Earth!" says Max.

Now Max the Little Monster never wastes ELECTRICITY.

He turns off lights except for the one he is using.

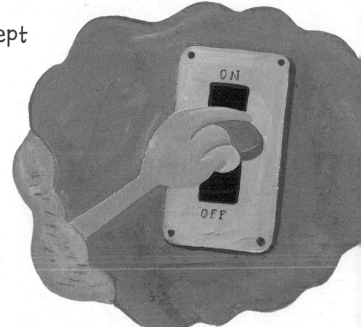

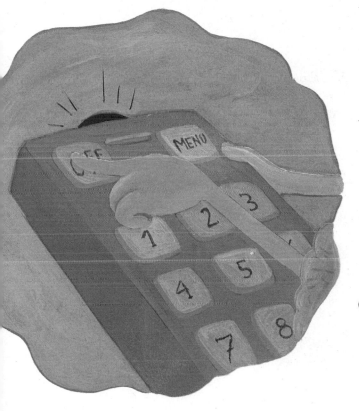

He hardly ever watches TV, but when he does, he turns it off when his program is over.

"Let's play outside!" says Max. "Fresh air feels **good** on my fur!"

Now Max the Little Monster never LITTERS. He RECYCLES any paper, aluminum cans, and plastic bottles he uses.

Max also likes to eat fresh fruits instead of candy, and drink water instead of soda pop. "Tasty," says Max. And he always throws his trash away in the right bin.

Max the Little Monster even has yard sales
where he sells all his old toys.

Max also trades his toys with his friends.
"**WOW!**" said Max. "Old toys I've never played
with before are just as fun as new toys!"

Now Max the Little Monster loves the Earth. He REDUCES the amount of water and energy he uses, he finds ways to REUSE as many things as he can, and he RECYCLES his trash.

Sometimes he even hugs trees.

KEEP THE WORLD BEAUTIFUL!

Max the Little Monster is now called Max the Little GREEN Monster.
You can be a little green monster, too, and help save the Earth!

MAX THE LITTLE GREEN MONSTER'S NEW WORDS

BLACKOUT: A power failure; when the electricity goes out.

COMPOST: A mixture of rotted leaves, plants, or vegetables that can be used in a garden to give nutrition to growing plants.

ELECTRICITY: The power used to make things like televisions, lights, and computers work.

GREEN: A word used to describe someone who is kind to the Earth and protects it from harm.

LITTER: To throw garbage away in places it does not belong, like on the ground or out of a car window.

POLLUTION: Things that make the environment dirty, like garbage, chemicals, or gases.

RECYCLE: To use trash to make new things.

REDUCE: To use less of something, like paper or electricity.

REUSE: To use something again in a different way instead of throwing it away.